What-a-Mess Goes to School

Frank Muir

Illustrated by Joseph Wright

PICTURE CORGI BOOKS

What-A-Mess Goes To School
A Picture Corgi Book 0 552 524050

Originally published in Great Britain in 1984 by A & C Black
(Publishers) Ltd.

PRINTING HISTORY
Picture Corgi edition published 1987

Picture Corgi Books are published by Transworld Publishers
Ltd., 61-63 Uxbridge Road, Ealing, London W5 5SA, in
Australia by Transworld Publishers (Australia) Pty. Ltd., 15-23
Helles Avenue, Moorebank, NSW 2170, and in New Zealand by
Transworld Publishers (N.Z.) Ltd., Cnr. Moselle and Waipareira
Avenues, Henderson, Auckland.

Made and printed in Portugal by Printer Portugesa

It was an unusually warm and sunny Sunday in March. The sort of day which makes everybody feel younger and happier.

Everybody, that is, except the puppy What-a-Mess.

The following morning he was going to school. For the first time.

School! Away from his mother! Among strangers! Not knowing how he was supposed to behave, where to go, what to do!

He howled when his mother told him. Just yelped and yelped until the humans who lived in his house thought he had hurt his paw and gave him a large piece of old cheese. He was very fond of food so he forgot all about school until he had eaten the cheese but then he remembered and the fear and sadness returned.

The family had gone off to church, taking his mother with them in the car, and What-a-Mess was curled up in what he called his Misery Hole. This was a hole in the middle of the compost heap which he dug whenever he was miserable. It was a bit smelly but was cosy and warm, and he was such a scruffy animal that nobody could tell which bit was puppy and which bit was compost so nobody knew he was there.

"I don't want to go to school tomorrow," he whimpered.
"I'm frightened of school. But what can I do?"

He had never felt so lonely in his life.

"If only I had *one* friend, just *one* fellow dog who
    would understand and . . . and . . ."

And then he remembered. He *did* have a friend. A strange little mongrel dog whom he had met at the seaside when he was on holiday.

"That's it!" What-a-Mess cried, leaping out of the compost. "I'll go and find my friend from the seaside. *He'll* understand and help me."

He had no idea where the seaside was but he reckoned that if he ran far enough he was bound to come to it. He knew it was a long way away so he decided to start immediately.

All Afghan hounds, even fat, lonely puppies like What-a-Mess, can jump well but the front gate looked frighteningly high. What-a-Mess backed away from the gate until his hindquarters were pressed against the fence at the bottom of the garden and he could back no further. Then, with a great bark to encourage himself, he began his run-up.

As he gathered speed and his coat streamed out behind him he looked like a greyhound wearing a fur-coat two sizes too big for him.

He was going like a rocket but he kept his eye on the gate and at exactly the right moment he went for lift-off and launched himself high into the air.

He cleared the gate easily. It was then, in mid-air, that he saw the bus. It was a huge bus and it was coming fast. Its horn was blaring as the driver tried to warn the puppy. But too late.

What-a-Mess did not make a graceful landing. He sort of splodged down on his tummy with all four legs spreadeagled. But he was travelling so fast that he shot across the road and the wheels of the bus missed him by a whisker.

He hit the opposite kerb, somersaulted into the air and came to rest against a fence, dazed and winded.

He was lying there, getting his breath back and wondering whether he had broken anything, when he felt an odd prickly feeling in his front legs and under his chin. And he heard a small voice say "You saved my life. Ta, very much. But for you I would've been squashed. Oh, yes. Bussed flat I would have been."

He looked down. Between his paws lay a little animal covered in spines. It had a very pink nose and tiny, very pink feet.

"It's the hot weather, that's the problem," said the voice. "Woke me up from my winter sleep too early. I got half way across the road and was too tired to go further so I lay down for a bit of a zizz. Saw the bus coming. Couldn't move. 'Bye-bye me' I thought. Then WHOOSH! You scooped me up just in time. I'm a hedgehog."

"How do you do," said What-a-Mess, who was still very dazed but had been well brought up. "My full name is What-a-Mess but my nickname is Prince Amir of Kinjan — no, the other way round."

"Oh no, I couldn't possibly call you Prince Amir of Kinjan No the Other Way Round. I'll just call you Watty."

"And may I ask your name?" said the puppy politely.

"Haven't got one."

What-a-Mess in his weak state suddenly felt terribly sorry about this.

"I'll give you one. Are you a boy or a girl?"

"I don't know. What's the difference?"

What-a-Mess thought. "I'm not sure. My mother is a girl so perhaps girls are the ones who have babies."

"Oh, I like that. Can I be a girl, please?"

"I suppose so. You talk more like a boy but if you like I'll call you Cynthia."

"Marvellous!" "Well, Watty . . ." said the hedgehog, eyelids drooping.

"Yes, Cynthia?" said the puppy.

"I must crawl back to my leaves in the wood and finish my winter sleep. I can't thank you enough for your heroic deed. Perhaps one day I'll be able to do the same for you. Cheerybye. All the best. Happy days . . ."

What-a-Mess watched the little hedgehog make its sleepy way along the fence and back towards the open country and then painfully and carefully he crossed the road to wait by the gate for the family to return.

Mrs Tibbett's Stables, Cattery, and Puppy Training Academy was only a few fields away so next morning What-a-Mess was walked there on a lead. At least that was the idea but he was in such a state of nerves that the little girl of the house had to pick him up and carry him. He chewed her hair all the way there.

There were eight other puppies in What-a-Mess's class but he was by far the youngest. The teacher was Mrs Wentworth-Blaze, a frighteningly large lady with a booming voice and huge red hands. When it came to What-a-Mess's turn for Obedience Training she dug her fingers into the small of his back and boomed "Siiiii-TTTT!" The puppy closed his eyes in terror and was sick into the top of her gumboot.

The puppies were awarded plus marks for things which they did well and minus marks for mistakes.

By Thursday it became clear that What-a-Mess did not understand anything which Mrs Wentworth-Blaze told him and was bottom of the class. His report card read:

Prince Amir of Kinjan. (Afghan Hound.)

PLUS MARKS: NIL.

MINUS MARKS:
On the command "stay" leaping forward
and nearly strangling himself on his choke
chain and having to be given the Kiss of
Life by the vet.

−10

Being given a cardboard identity card
reading "4" to wear on his collar and
eating it.

−6

−8

Disappearing before Mrs Wentworth-
Blaze's lesson on "Obeying the Whistle"
and being found hiding behind a chicken.

Persistently biting the tail of the dog in front during "Walking Proudly In a Circle" practice.

−9

−35

After four days of tuition failing to understand any of the following commands: Sit. Stand. Lie down. Get up. Stay. Go. To Heel. Fetch. Seek. Walkies. (etc.)

During "Walking to Heel on the Lead" practice, on the command "Sit" running round and round Mrs Wentworth-Blaze

so that the lead bound her legs tightly together causing her to topple over.

−500

Total to date: Minus 568 marks.

But What-a-Mess did not mind being bottom of the class. To his surprise he found that school, apart from the lessons, was terrific fun. During playtime all the puppies mucked about in a field and What-a-Mess was very popular with the others because he was the best at inventing games.

One of his friends was a clever little terrier who told What-a-Mess not to bother with trying to understand what was shouted at him but to follow close behind and just copy what the terrier did. What-a-Mess began to get a little better at the exercises.

"Oh, mother," he said on the Thursday evening, "why didn't you *tell* me that school would be so enjoyable. It's *much* nicer than hanging round the house with nobody to play with."

Then came the shock.

The next morning all the puppies were lined up and told that it was time for their exams. Each puppy was to be given a different Initiative Test. Any puppy who failed the test would have to leave the school immediately.

What-a-Mess was in despair. As each test was different he could not copy what his terrier friend did. He could not bear to watch as the other puppies happily fetched things to the whistle and obeyed commands and walked on the lead without pulling and all the other clever things which What-a-Mess could never do. He could only hope against hope that his test would be an easy one.

It was not an easy one. For an Afghan with a very sharp nose and no sense of direction it was impossible. There was a plank of wood propped up in the grass. It had a little doorway cut into it. What-a-Mess was given an old leather cricket-ball. His task was to nose the ball through the doorway in thirty seconds. He tried, of course.

He gave the ball a big push with his nose in the direction of the plank but the ball was heavy and would not go straight. It rolled away to one side each time he pushed. Furious with it he got his nose under the ball and gave a great heave. The ball sailed through the air and fell to the ground behind the plank. Racing against time, What-a-Mess galloped round to retrieve it.

There, behind the plank, lay the cricket ball. And beside it stood a little spiny creature, about the same colour, except for tiny pink feet and a little pink nose.

What-a-Mess blinked. "Cynthia!" he gulped.

"What-ho, Watty!" said the little hedgehog. "My turn to do *you* a good deed. Quick! Give me a push! And she rolled herself into a tight ball.

What-a-Mess gave the hedgehog a little nudge with his nose and it rolled swiftly round the board, straightened up and came to a halt close to the doorway. What-a-Mess bounded after it.

The hedgehog unrolled slightly.

"So I can see where I'm going," she explained. "One more push, please!"

What-a-Mess gave another little nudge. The hedgehog ball rolled sideways as the cricket ball had done but turned sharply left towards the hole, moved a little right to correct the swing and, to excited barks from all What-a-Mess's friends, rolled triumphantly through the doorway.

What-a-Mess was too excited to sleep that night. He lay in his basket thinking, and rather noisily chewing a new bone which he had been given by the family for passing his test and being accepted by the school. Beside him in his basket was a saucer of milk. He heard the cat-door flap open and a few moments later there was a prickly feeling in the paw which was next to the saucer. He looked down and a small pink nose was in the milk.

"I can't get to sleep for the noise you're making with that bone" his mother said a little crossly. "I think the most important thing in your life is food."

"No," said the puppy. "It's friends. Well, friends *and* food. Or perhaps it's food and then friends. It's difficult to say which comes first but on the whole I'd say . . ."

But What-a-Mess never did say. He fell asleep instead.